Honoring Different Cultures

UNDERSTANDING CITIZENSHIP

Vanessa Flores

CIVICS FOR THE REAL WORLD™

Rosen Classroom™

People around the world have different beliefs and ways of life. These different ways of life make up a person's culture!

There are many different cultures around the world. You might even have friends at school from different cultures.

You might learn about other cultures in social studies class. Maps and globes show where all the countries of the world are.

In Chinese culture, people eat a lot of rice. Instead of using forks, they eat with chopsticks.

In American culture, people love football. In many other cultures around the world, *fútbol*—or soccer—is the most popular sport!

Dancing is an important part of Irish culture. Dancers often curl their hair and wear beautiful dresses.

In Germany, some children start school when they're three years old. Parents give children paper cones full of presents on the first day of school.

There are many different cultures around the world. There are even different cultures in the United States!

You can learn about other cultures by reading books. You can also talk to other people about their cultures.

By honoring different cultures, we can see what makes people different. We can also see what makes people the same!

WORDS TO KNOW

book

chopsticks

globe

map